by ELSE HOLMELUND MINARIK

THE LITTLE

AND THE

HARPER & ROW, PUBLISHERS

Text copyright © 1963 by Else Holmelund Minarik
Pictures copyright © 1963 by Garth Williams

Printed in the United States of America. All rights reserved.
Library of Congress catalog card number: 63-19681

PICTURES BY GARTH WILLIAMS

GIANT GIRL
ELF BOY

NEW YORK, EVANSTON, AND LONDON

Listen—

There was once a little giant girl.
Her mother sent her out to pick
something for the table.
"Pick a nice little bush," said her mother,
"—a nice little bush with flowers.
That will look pretty on the table."

So the little giant girl went out
to pick a nice little bush with flowers
for the table.

Now—

There was also a little elf boy.
His mother sent him out to pick
something for the table.
"Pick a nice little bud,"
said his mother,
"—a nice little bud and one nice
little leaf, perhaps.
That will look pretty on the table."

So the little elf boy went out
to pick a nice little bud
and a very small leaf
to look pretty on the table.

He found a bush with flowers.
He climbed it for fun.

Then along came the little giant girl,
and she picked the bush,

and she took it home to her mother,

and they put it in a vase
on the table.

"Ooh—" said the little giant girl.
"Look here, Mother!"

She had found the elf.

"My goodness—a little elf!" said her mother, and smiled.

"You must take him back where you found him."

So the little giant girl very gently
took the elf back where she
had found the bush.

There she put him down.

"If I could grow little," she said,
"we might be playmates."

He nodded and smiled.

"But I can't grow little," she said,
"and you can't grow big—"

He shook his head.

He made a bow.

He blew a kiss

and ran home to his mother.

"Oh, dear," sighed the little giant girl.
"Ah, well.
But we can't all be the same size, can we?
If I were elf-size,
just think of all the elf steps
I'd have to take to get home.
Just think!
One hundred million at least."

And with that happy thought
she danced over the hills,
taking lovely big giant steps all the way.